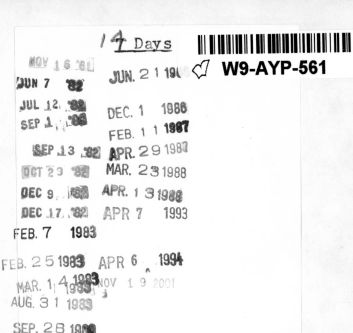

Quarter Horse Winner

Elizabeth Van Steenwyk

Illustrated by Susan Mohn

Albert Whitman & Company, Chicago

Library of Congress Cataloging in Publication Data
Van Steenwyk, Elizabeth.
    Quarter horse winner.

    (A Springboard book)
    SUMMARY: As she strives for a place on the Midtown
Stables gymkhana team, 13-year-old Holly gradually
becomes more sensitive to the needs of other people and
of her horse.
    [1. Horses—Fiction] I. Mohn, Susan. II. Title.
PZ7.V358Qar   [Fic]   79-28490
ISBN 0-8075-6707-8

            Text © 1980 by Elizabeth Van Steenwyk
    Illustrations © 1980 by Albert Whitman & Company
            Published simultaneously in Canada
            by General Publishing, Limited, Toronto
            All rights reserved. Printed in U.S.A.

Contents

1
At the Stables

Holly Flynn stood in a stall at Midtown Stables and concentrated hard on the rippling coat of her quarter horse gelding. She brushed and stroked in a strong rhythm that made the dust fly off in clouds.

"Like that, do you, Buddy Boy?" she said. As if in answer, he pulled a mouthful of hay from his trough and began to chew with a slow, steady crunch.

"That's it, enjoy it all." Holly paused to catch

her breath. "The rubdown, the feed, the snooze that's coming. You're tired from the workout, I know."

Holly wiped her forehead with the sleeve of her plaid shirt and looked around the barn. This was the best time of day, when the late August sun crept low and shadows that looked like dirty stall blankets gathered in the far corners of the building. Most of the kids were still out on the trails with their horses, so she and Buddy had the moldy, smelly barn all to themselves. Holly liked being alone with Buddy, liked talking to him out loud and watching his ears flip back and forth as if he understood every word.

She felt slightly self-conscious about talking to him like this, however. Ten-year-olds talked to their horses in the movies, but thirteen-year-olds in Bakersfield, California, were supposed to act more grown-up.

Holly put her hand on Buddy's jaw and felt the muscles move up and down as he continued to chew. "We've got to talk some more about our workouts, Buddy," she said. "You've acted so jumpy lately, and you won't follow directions. Sometimes I think you don't like to perform. I know there are some horses who aren't great athletes, and I don't care if you aren't great. But I do want you to be good enough to enter the pole-bending event in a couple of weeks."

Holly stroked Buddy's neck. She knew that Mrs. Owens, the owner of Midtown Stables, would be choosing her gymkhana team for the county fair soon. If she and Buddy didn't improve, they'd never be able to represent Midtown at the fair.

"We've got to start working harder, Buddy," Holly said. "The fair's opening in three weeks, and we don't have much time left."

Suddenly, Holly heard a noise near the stall entrance. She jumped against Buddy and looked around. A face darted out of sight as long brown hair fanned the corridor air.

"Hey," Holly shouted. "Come back here."

"Oh...I'm sorry." Tess Bundy peered

around the corner of the doorway, her look serious and intense behind thick glasses. "I didn't mean to bother you."

"You're not bothering me," Holly said. "Just don't creep up on me that way again."

"I thought...well, I thought I heard voices, and I was only going to peek..."

"I was thinking out loud," Holly said. "That's all."

Holly wondered if Tess would understand how she had to talk to her horse sometimes. Probably not. Most people wouldn't.

"Could you tell me...I mean, may I ask you...something?" Tess said hesitantly.

"Sure," Holly said. "What do you want to know?"

"Why do you have that stuffed rabbit here in the stall?" Tess pointed to the flop-eared, dirty yellow rabbit sitting on a corner shelf.

Holly began to laugh. "Oh, that's Buddy's mascot. He gets lonesome sometimes."

"Horses get lonesome, too?" Tess looked as though she didn't believe it.

"Sure do," Holly said. "Lots of horses have mascots. Some racehorses have live ones, like goats or ducks."

"No kidding," Tess said. "I didn't know that."

"But Buddy just likes this old rabbit near him in the stall. I'm glad he didn't settle on an elephant or giraffe to be best friends with." Holly went back to brushing Buddy's mane.

"There is one other thing..." Tess began.

Holly turned around again. "Do you need a ride home? I came on my bike, so I can't..."

"No, I don't need a ride," Tess said. "I wanted to ask about the meeting Mrs. Owens has called for tomorrow."

"Oh, you mean about the riding team?" Holly couldn't imagine Tess wanting to try out for the team. She was always such a loner. She never joined the other kids in the ring or stood around and laughed and talked with them after riding. No one had gotten to know her, even though she'd been coming to the stables all summer.

"Yes, I thought I might...well, join, or whatever it is you do." Tess took a hesitant step into the hall.

"Mrs. Owens will explain about tryouts tomorrow," Holly said.

"Oh, I see." Tess picked at a thread on her T-shirt. "Is it...um...all right if I come?"

"Of course, Tess. You don't need an invitation trimmed in gold or anything. It's just a meeting."

"Will there be a lot of people there?"

"Probably." Holly began to pack her brushes away in the tack box. "Tell you what, why don't you come with me? The meeting's to be at one o'clock in Mrs. Owens's office."

"All right," Tess said. "I'll go with you, that is if it's really okay."

"Of course it is," Holly said. "I'll meet you outside Mrs. Owens's office."

Tess smiled, and the light in her eyes beamed right through her glasses. What was Tess so happy about? Holly wondered. It was nothing but an old meeting.

"See you tomorrow." Tess waved, disappearing into the shadowy aisle between the stalls.

Holly whispered goodbye to Buddy Boy and closed the rugged stall door. Then she hurried outside, crossed the stableyard, and unlocked her bike in the rack. After she had hopped on, she headed toward the gravel path that led to the main street and home.

Ten minutes later, Holly turned into her own driveway. She parked her bike in the garage between the power mower and her dad's golf cart. Then she stepped into the kitchen, just in time to hear her mother end a telephone conversation in the other room. A second later, Holly's mother appeared in the kitchen doorway.

"Holly, I thought I heard you out here." Mrs. Flynn went over to the stove and began to stir something in a pan. Holly looked closely at her. Had she been crying?

"What's the matter, Mom?"

"It's your Aunt Helen, honey. She's in the hospital. Uncle Frank just called to say she's going to have an operation in the morning."

"Will she be all right?"

Holly's mother turned to face her. "Eventually, but she'll have to be in the hospital for at least three weeks."

"What about Chad? Who's going to take care of him?" Holly asked about her five-year-old cousin.

"We are." Her mother's eyes brightened. "Uncle Frank is putting him on a plane first thing in the morning. Won't that be nice? You'll be able to teach Chad to ride Buddy Boy."

"Sure," Holly said. "That's nice." But she didn't mean it. How could she train Buddy with Chad underfoot for the next three weeks? How would she ever make the team now?

2
Hurt Feelings

Holly was in a bad mood the next day when she went with her mother to the airport. She had wanted to spend the morning training Buddy, but now that was impossible. There was even a good chance she would miss the meeting.

Fortunately, Chad's plane was on time. It touched down just after noon, and Chad was the first one off. He hurried down the steps of the plane carrying three paper airplanes and an orange football helmet. His raincoat trailed on the steps behind him.

His eyes were bright with excitement as he ran toward Holly and her mother. "I had a hamburger and two cokes for lunch," he announced. "And the lady sitting next to me didn't want her dessert, so I ate that, too."

A stewardess came up to them and handed Mrs. Flynn Chad's ticket.

"Then I got to go with the stewardess to see where the pilot sits," Chad went on. "After that, we made paper airplanes. It sure is hotter here than it is in Philadelphia."

"Bye, Chad." The stewardess breathed a sigh of relief. "He has two suitcases," she called back as she hurried away.

Mrs. Flynn bent down and kissed Chad's freckled cheek. Holly hoped that she wouldn't have to do that, but she didn't need to worry. Chad backed away from his aunt and quickly wiped his face.

"Aunt Martha, can I go barefoot?" he asked as they headed for the baggage claim section.

"We'll see," Mrs. Flynn said. "What color are your suitcases?"

"Purple, I think. Or maybe green." He dropped his football helmet on the floor.

"Holly, please help him, will you?" Mrs. Flynn went to watch for Chad's suitcases.

Holly picked up Chad's helmet and his raincoat, which he had dropped next. Then he dropped his paper airplanes while she tried to hand him his raincoat. She could see having Chad around was going to be a lot of fun. "I'll carry your helmet and raincoat," Holly said.

"How's Buddy Boy?" Chad asked.

"How do you know about him?" Holly wondered. She flicked her dark braids off her shoulders.

"Remember, you told me about him on the telephone last Christmas. Your folks gave him to you, and you said it was the neatest present you'd ever had in your whole life."

Yes, Holly remembered. She'd just about given up ever having a horse of her very own, and then, the day before Christmas, her mom and dad had taken her to Midtown Stables and there was Buddy.

"When do I get to ride him?" Chad pulled on her jeans. "I can already ride a pony."

"Real soon," Holly said, glancing anxiously at the clock on the wall. It was nearly time for the riding team meeting, and she'd promised to meet Tess and sit with her. Maybe Tess would go inside Mrs. Owens's office without her. Holly hurried over to her mother.

"Mom, can you drop me off at the stables on the way home? I have this meeting..."

"I thought we'd have some lunch first."

"Chad doesn't need any more to eat."

Her mother laughed. "You're right. Let's go, Chad."

Fifteen minutes later, Holly ran into Mrs. Owens's office at the stables. "Sorry I'm late," she said to the room full of girls and Mrs. Owens, and especially to Tess, over in the corner.

"We're late today, too, Holly," Mrs. Owens said. "Find a chair and we'll begin."

Holly sat down and looked around. All the best riders at the stables were here.

Mrs. Owens rapped on her desk with a bronze horseshoe. "As you all know, we're here to talk about the selection of the gymkhana riding team. It's too bad that you all can't be on it, but unfortunately there isn't room. That's why I'm holding tryouts for the various positions in two weeks. I'll be selecting the best pole benders, best barrel racers . . . the best two people in every event."

Tess raised her hand timidly.

"Yes, Tess, what is it?" Mrs. Owens asked.

"What . . . um . . . what is gymkhana?" She blushed.

The group broke out into a flurry of giggles.

"Simmer down, everyone," Mrs. Owens warned. "Tess hasn't had the experience that most of you have had, so we owe her an explanation. Would anyone care to help me out?"

Karen Blair raised her hand. "A gymkhana is a fun day of games on horseback."

"There's a lot more to it than that," Judy Holmes said. "The games are separated into timed and speed events. You and your horse have to practice hard to do well."

"You're both right," Mrs. Owens said. "It's a fun day, but it's also a day to show what you've learned about horsemanship, excuse me, horsewomanship."

Everyone laughed. Mrs. Owens waited until the group had quieted down. Then she went on. "In two weeks, we're going to decide who will be on the team at the county fair. Those of you who want to compete for a place may do so. Remember, however, that we already have many top competitors for the barrel racing event, so if your time isn't excellent in it, you'd better try out for something else. As I said, I'll only be taking two girls in each of seven events, so pick your best one and practice hard."

As Holly stood up, the talk buzzed around her. She wondered whether she should pick pole bending, after all. Could she and Buddy solve their problem in just two weeks? Pole bending *was* the most exciting event next to barrel racing, and Buddy did seem to have the balance and coordination for it. Well, she'd go ahead and pick pole bending. She and Buddy would just work harder.

"Holly."

She turned and looked straight into Tess's glasses. They were thicker than she'd first noticed.

"What is it, Tess?"

"What event are you going to enter?"

"Pole bending," Holly answered.

"Maybe I'll try that, too," Tess said as they headed toward the door.

"Have you ridden much?" Holly asked. It had just occurred to her that she had never actually seen Tess ride a horse.

Tess cleared her throat. "Oh, some."

"You must have ridden English then."

"Oh, no," Tess said. "I've never been to England."

Holly began to laugh. "You don't have to go to England to ride English," she said. "That's just a style of riding." Holly couldn't hold back the giggles. They burst out of her, uncontrolled.

"I...I didn't know." Tess looked more embarrassed than ever.

"What's so funny?" Karen Blair asked.

Holly wiped her eyes. "I think Tess is teasing us. You know what she said?" Holly repeated Tess's remark, and Karen began to giggle, too.

"Hey, Judy," Karen shouted. "Listen to what Tess said."

"I'll see you later," Tess said suddenly to Holly, as Judy joined in the laughter.

"Okay." Holly shook her head. "I don't believe it. I just don't believe it."

Tess disappeared, and Holly went inside the stable.

"Come on, Buddy," she whispered, opening his stall door. "We've got work to do. You're about to become the champion pole bender's favorite partner."

Buddy turned to look at her and nickered softly as she rubbed his velvety nose. Holly stood in the earthy warmth of the small room, patting and stroking Buddy as he started to nuzzle her hair.

"Stop that," Holly said. "You're tickling me."

Then she heard a strange muffled noise, a sound that seemed out of place in the barn. "Shh," she whispered, holding Buddy's head still.

The noise came again, like a strangled sob.

"I'll be right back," Holly whispered, closing the stall door behind her.

She followed the sound. It seemed to be coming from the third stall down the corridor. But whose stall was it? Holly tried to slip in quietly, but the door creaked as it swung open.

A beautiful bay quarter horse stood inside, its ears moving back and forth in alarm. A girl sat on the floor, sobbing.

"Tess!" Holly cried. "What's the matter?"

Tess looked up, her eyes full of tears. Her glasses lay on the floor beside her. "Nothing," she said. She put her glasses on quickly and wiped at her eyes.

Suddenly, Holly understood. Oh, no, she thought. Tess wasn't teasing. She didn't know what English riding was!

3
Rude Friends

Holly sat silently at the dining room table, pushing green beans into a row on her plate. She listened to her cousin's voice babble on and on. Chad was okay for a little kid, Holly guessed, but his constant talking got on her nerves. Sometimes she just had to tune him out.

"Holly, eat your beans," her mother interrupted Chad.

"I ate all mine, Aunt Martha."

"Is everything all right down at the stables, Holly?" her father asked. "You haven't talked about Buddy for a couple of days."

"Yes, fine," Holly said, though she didn't mean it. She had had several more practice sessions with Buddy during the past two days but hadn't made any progress. He kept refusing to obey when she tried to take him around the poles. The worst thing was, she didn't know what was wrong.

"Holly, you're a million miles away," her mother said. "Come on, help me with the dishes."

Holly followed her mother into the kitchen.

"I hope you won't mind taking care of Chad again tomorrow." Mrs. Flynn put some dirty dishes into the sink. "You know I've had this luncheon planned for several days. Maybe you could take him down to the stables. I'm sure he'd enjoy that."

"Yes, but Mom...what can I do with him there? I've got to work out. Buddy's not performing well, and I need to practice."

"Just take care of Chad tomorrow," her mother pleaded. "Please?"

"Well, okay." Holly sighed. Since Chad had arrived, she had had to spend most of her free time entertaining him. She might not mind it so much if she weren't worried about Buddy. But as it was, she needed all the extra time she could get.

"You know," Mrs. Flynn said, breaking the silence, "I'm concerned about Chad. I think he's terribly worried about his mother, and yet he's never mentioned her to me. When I told him her surgery was successful, he changed the subject and started talking about something else."

"He sure is a non-stop talker," Holly said. "I'm going to need some earplugs."

Her mother smiled. "Holly, has Chad talked about his mother with you?"

"No," Holly admitted. "I guess that's funny, isn't it?"

Mrs. Flynn scrubbed the last pan. "Some people manage to hide things deep inside them," she said. "Sometimes the things that bother them most are the things they talk least about."

"How do you ever find out what's bothering them?" Holly asked.

"By caring...by listening..."

Holly felt a twinge of guilt. Since Chad had arrived, she hadn't really listened to him. She had been too wrapped up in her own concerns. Poor Chad. He probably was homesick.

Chad rushed into the kitchen. "Uncle Bill said he'd buy us an ice-cream cone for dessert if you'd walk me down to the Tasty Queen, Holly."

"You're on," she said. "You want some ice cream, Mom?"

"I'd better skip it. Thanks, anyway."

As Holly and Chad walked down the street in the twilight, she felt his small hand creep inside hers. "Talk to me, Holly," he said. "Tell me about Buddy Boy."

"Wouldn't you rather talk about your mom, Chad?" Holly asked gently.

"No," Chad said. "Tell me about Buddy Boy."

Well, at least I tried, Holly thought. "What do you want to know?"

"Will he like me?"

"Sure. Buddy never met a stranger."

"What kind of horse is he?"

"He's a quarter horse."

"Does that mean you paid a quarter for him?"

"No," Holly laughed. "That name comes from Colonial times. People built their own little race courses at home and invited their friends to race their horses. The length of their course, or track, was only a quarter of a mile. Then the owners developed a type of horse that would run this track and called him a quarter horse."

"Who told you all that stuff?" Chad began to skip now.

"I read it in a book somewhere. I read a lot about horses."

"What do you and Buddy do at the stables?" Chad asked.

"We're training for a tryout that's being held in about two weeks."

"What are you going to do in the tryout?"

"We're going to be in the pole-bending event."

Chad's laughter filled the quiet evening air. "Pole bending? That sounds really dumb."

Holly laughed, too, as she realized how funny the words must sound to her little cousin. "It's fun, Chad."

"But how does a horse bend a pole?"

"The horse doesn't bend any poles, silly," Holly said. "But you could say he bends himself. He has to be limber...flexible..."

"What does that mean?"

"Nimble," Holly said.

"Oh, like 'Jack be nimble, Jack be quick'?" Chad asked.

"Right." Holly gave his hand a squeeze. "Buddy has to be quick and able to gallop around the poles that are set up in the arena. If we touch a pole, or worse, knock one down, time is added to our score. And the whole idea is to have the lowest score, not the highest."

"I'll help you tomorrow." Chad skipped a couple of steps. Then he spotted the bright lights of the ice-cream store. "Look, we're there." Releasing her hand, he darted ahead and ran inside. Holly hurried now, too, as she saw a group of kids from the stables standing near the entrance.

"Hi, Holly," Karen Blair said. "Want to go to the movies with us?"

"Sure, but I'll have to go home and ask first." She opened the door for Chad. "I'll just be a few minutes," she said to the girls.

As Holly stepped into the crowded, noisy room, she saw Tess standing in a far corner. Tess hadn't been at the stables for a couple of days, Holly suddenly realized. But, then, Holly had been so busy with Chad and worried about Buddy's performance that she hadn't had much time to think about Tess. Tess saw her but quickly turned away.

Holly knew that she had to go up and say something to her. But what?

"I want plain chocolate." Chad was pulling on her arm.

"Just a minute, Chad." Holly grabbed him and pulled him with her toward Tess.

"Hi, Tess. We've missed you down at the stables. I didn't know you lived around here."

"About six blocks away. But I've never come here before." Tess looked at Chad, and her face softened. "You're lucky to have a little brother."

"I'm not her brother," Chad spoke up. "I'm her cousin, and I'm visiting from Philadelphia."

"That's nice," Tess said. "I mean, I guess it's nice, isn't it?"

"Have you ever been to Philadelphia?" Chad asked Tess. Before she could say anything, he continued. "It's a real neat place."

"I'll get our ice cream," Holly said. She had a feeling Chad was on one of his talking marathons again.

She was right. When she came back five minutes later, he was still talking. And Tess was actually listening. Amazing!

"Here's your plain chocolate cone," Holly said to Chad. Then she turned to Tess. "I bought you one, too, Tess. Double fudge ripple, my favorite."

"Oh, thanks," Tess said, "but you didn't have to do that."

"Oh, yes she did." Chad spoke up between licks. "It wouldn't be polite for us to eat in front of you."

Tess smiled at him as she began to eat her ice cream.

"Guess we'd better head for home," Holly said, remembering her invitation to the movies.

"Do we have to go?" Chad said. "I want to talk to Tess some more. She's my new friend."

"You'll be seeing her down at the stables." Holly started slowly for the door, and Tess and Chad followed.

"Good," Chad said. "We'll ride horses all day, Tess."

"I don't know," Tess said.

They were outside now, on the sidewalk in

front of the ice-cream store. Holly looked at the cluster of girls who had asked her to go to the movies.

"Be right back," she told Chad and Tess. She walked over to the girls. "I've got to take my little cousin home..."

Judy Holmes interrupted her. "I hope you're not planning to ask Tess to go with us."

Holly felt her back stiffen and was surprised at her own reaction. "Why not?"

"Because she asks such dumb questions," Judy said.

"Like the one she asked in Mrs. Owens's office!" Karen said. "I couldn't believe it!"

"And that comment about English riding!" Judy said. "She probably doesn't even know how to ride. Well, have you ever seen her on a horse?" The girls started to giggle.

Holly glanced at Tess, afraid that she had overheard Judy and Karen. Fortunately, Tess was busy laughing at something Chad had told her.

"No," Holly answered Judy. "I wasn't

planning to ask Tess. And I just remembered I can't go with you. Thanks, anyway."

She turned and walked back to Tess and Chad, trying to fight down her anger. Judy and Karen could be so mean!

"Okay, it's all settled," she announced with forced enthusiasm. "We're going on a trail ride tomorrow. We'll rent a pony for Chad, and I'll bring lunch. See you first thing in the morning, Tess."

Holly grabbed Chad by the hand and turned down the walk toward home.

Maybe Tess didn't know a lot about riding, Holly thought, but she was willing to learn. It wasn't right for people to be so rude!

4
Worried

Holly tried to look cheerful when she and Chad met Tess at the stables the next morning. Maybe she wouldn't have time to practice, but at least she'd be able to ride Buddy.

She looked at Tess, who was holding the reins of a chestnut-colored mare as if they were snakes ready to bite.

All of a sudden, something clicked in Holly's head. "Haven't you ever ridden a horse?" she asked in disbelief.

"No," Tess said softly.

Holly couldn't believe her own ears. "Then

why have you been coming to the stables all this time?"

"Can we go?" Chad asked. His pony stomped impatiently.

"Only if you promise not to let your pony gallop." Holly brushed her braids off her shoulders. "Wait for us down at the first fork in the trail." Chad's pony took off toward the path.

"Why have you been coming to the stables all summer?" Holly asked Tess again.

"Promise you won't laugh?"

Holly felt her face flush. "Yes, Tess, I promise."

"I don't live far from here. In fact, I can see the stables from my house." Tess gave Holly a shy glance.

"That's neat," Holly said.

"I guess it is. I didn't have anything special to do, so I just came over here."

"Why didn't you take riding lessons or something?" Holly asked. "You would have had a lot more fun."

"I . . . I don't know." Tess scuffed her feet and stirred up some dust. "Mrs. Owens said it was all right for me to be here and take my time about learning to ride."

"Whose horse is this?" Holly gave the chestnut a pat.

"It belongs to the stable. Mrs. Owens says Alice is the gentlest horse she's got." Tess drew a deep breath. "I sure hope she's right."

Holly shook her head impatiently. "Don't be afraid. Come on, I'll give you a lift up."

Holly was glad that none of the other girls were around as Tess struggled to mount the patient horse. They would have laughed for sure, and Tess didn't need that. She needed encouragement right now.

"There," Holly said. "Hang on to the reins and tell your horse to gidday-up by squeezing her sides with the calves of your legs. She'll take right off for the trail."

"Holly," Tess said, almost in a whisper. "Maybe I'll wait until another day."

"No, you won't." Holly gave Alice's hip a

soft slap. "You're going to try it, or my name isn't Holly Flynn."

Alice began a slow, steady walk through the barnyard and across the field to the trail. Holly mounted Buddy Boy and clicked him into a trot so that he soon caught up with Tess and Alice. Holly felt the lunch in her day pack bounce in rhythm with Buddy's smooth gait.

"See, what did I tell you?" Holly said. "Nothing to it, is there?"

But when Tess turned to look at her, Holly saw that her face was pinched into a terrified mask.

Before Holly could think of something to say to reassure her, she saw Chad returning. "What's the matter?" she asked.

"I don't have anybody to talk to when I'm alone," Chad began. "And I like to talk."

"So I've noticed." Holly laughed. Then she added, "Why don't you talk to Tess while we're riding?"

Chad pulled his pony to a stop so that it blocked the path. Now they were all forced to halt. "You want me to talk to you, Tess?" Chad asked.

Tess glanced down at the reins in her hands. "Well...um...yes."

"What's the matter?" Chad squinted into the sun as he stared at her.

"I'm scared," Tess admitted.

"Well, don't worry." Chad sat straighter in his saddle. "I'm here now. Everything'll be okay."

Tess looked up, first at Chad, then at Holly. A shadow of a smile played across her face, and the scrunched-up tightness in her shoulders seemed to loosen a little.

Good old Chad, Holly thought. Sometimes he says the right thing. She looked at her cousin with new appreciation.

"Let's play follow the leader," Holly said. "You go first, Chad, then Tess. I'll be last. After a while, it will be Tess's turn to be first."

Chad's eyes brightened as he turned the pony around and headed down the trail into the woods. Alice sauntered along behind the

pony, and Holly and Buddy crept down the path behind them.

Holly stopped worrying about Tess and began to think about Buddy. She tried not to fidget but couldn't help herself. If only she could figure out what Buddy's problem was! Why couldn't he behave as well in the practice ring as he did on the trail? What was bothering him?

5

In the Center Ring

A few days later, Holly led Buddy out of the stable to the yard where Chad and Tess were waiting.

"This will be my second time on the trail this morning," Tess said. Her eyes shone behind her glasses.

"Second time?" Holly asked. "But it's only nine-thirty. Who did you go with the first time?"

"Nobody, except Alice, of course." Tess

paused to look at Chad, who was giggling. "I got here before eight and Mrs. Owens said it was okay to take Alice out for a spin."

"Bet you put her saddle on backwards," Chad said.

"You can't expect me to do everything right in just a few days." Tess pretended to be angry, but her smile gave her away.

"Wow, I'm really impressed," Holly said.

Tess was changing rapidly, almost before Holly's eyes. Of course, sitting on a horse like Alice didn't require too much skill. All you had to do was put one leg on each side and your mind in the middle, as Holly's first riding teacher used to say. But to conquer fear was really something. Tess was a brave person.

"Let's go, Holly," Chad said.

"Just need to cinch up my stirrups a little," Holly replied. "You and Tess can start, if you like. I'll catch up."

"Okay," Tess said. "Come on, Chad." Tess led the way to the trail.

"Holly," someone called to her. She turned

to see Karen hurrying toward her from the barn. "Where are you going?"

"Out on the trail with Tess and Chad." Holly was still a little angry with Judy and Karen.

"Judy and I thought you might want to ride with us this morning."

"Thanks," Holly said, softening. "But I promised Tess and Chad I'd ride with them. You're welcome to come with us."

"Well..." Karen looked at Tess and Chad, who had already started down the trail. "I don't know if I want to ride with Tess. It can't be any fun riding with a beginner."

"You've got a rotten attitude, Karen." Holly's temper flared. "Everybody is a beginner sometime."

Karen looked at Holly with surprise. "I guess you're right," she said slowly. "I was a terrible rider at first."

Holly scratched Buddy's ears before she replied. "I wasn't very good either. But I wasn't as bad as you were."

Karen laughed. "Okay, I take the prize for

being the worst rider of the year. We'll catch up with you guys as soon as Judy gets Ginger saddled."

Holly prepared to mount Buddy as Karen went on. "I have noticed one thing about Tess these last few days since you started helping her. One thing besides her riding, I mean. She's changing or something. It's her attitude, I think. She's a lot friendlier. And it's just since she started riding Alice."

"And started making friends," Holly added. "Mainly me and Chad so far, though, and no one else."

Holly hoped her hint wouldn't be lost on Karen. It wasn't.

"You're right." Karen stirred up some dust with the toe of her boot. "I guess we weren't very nice to her that night at the ice-cream store. You have to admit she said some pretty stupid things—like that remark about English riding. But I'm not very proud of myself." She smiled shyly at Holly.

"Give you a lift up?" Karen offered.

"Sure," Holly said, smiling back at her. Maybe Karen, who was an expert rider, could help her figure out what was wrong with Buddy. She frowned as she thought about her problem with him.

"Hey, space case." Karen gave her a poke. "I only offered to help you mount up. You look as if I asked you to solve the problems of the world."

"I was thinking about Buddy and his contrariness," Holly said. "I'm worried about how well he'll do during tryouts."

"Listen, you'll figure Buddy out." Karen's voice was confident. "You're a terrific rider, you really are."

"Then why is Buddy refusing to go around the poles if I'm such a great rider? I'm supposed to be in charge, not him."

"He's not sick, is he? Not off his feed?"

"No, nothing like that." Holly chewed her lip.

Karen thought a moment. "Why don't you ask Mrs. Owens?"

"She's so busy," Holly said. "But maybe I will." As she hurried to catch up with Tess and Chad, she realized why she hadn't asked Mrs. Owens to help her before this. If Mrs. Owens knew she was having so much trouble, she might not want her on the team. Holly hoped she could solve the problem alone, without Mrs. Owens knowing about it.

Karen and Judy rode with Holly, Chad, and Tess until eleven-thirty. Holly, Tess, and Chad continued riding and at noon stopped for lunch among the trees. They tied their horses, then sat down in the tall grass and broke open the day pack.

Tess sighed and took a long drink from Holly's thermos. "I think riding is fun," she said, wiping her mouth on her sleeve. She bit into a generous peanut-butter sandwich.

"Why were you scared of horses?" Chad asked.

"Chad, you shouldn't ask things like that," Holly said. She handed a piece of celery to him.

"That's okay," Tess said. She swallowed

before she went on. "It's just that I've always been scared about doing new things. Scared of my own shadow half the time."

"Are you *still* scared?" Chad asked.

"No," Tess said, smiling at him. "Not anything like I was a few days ago."

"What did I tell you?" Holly said. "Once you've got a little experience at riding, you'll find out that horses don't bite." She started to laugh before she added, "very much."

Tess began to laugh, too. They ate their lunches while Chad ran after a butterfly in the meadow just beyond the trees. The horses swished their tails and nibbled on some tall grass. A bird high above them warbled a noontime song. Holly leaned against a tree and realized she was having a good time, though she hadn't expected it. Trail rides were fun. There were no pressures on her or the horse as there were in training or competing for a place on the team. And it was especially fun being with Tess. Why hadn't they gotten to know one another sooner?

"Tess," Holly said. "I've been meaning to ask you something. That night at the ice-cream store you said you lived in the area, but I've never seen you at school."

"That's because I've always gone to a private school across town. Mom teaches kindergarten there, so when I was little, it was easier to go with her than to another school." Tess helped herself to another peanut-butter sandwich and some carrot sticks. "But in the fall, I'm transferring to public school. I'm going to junior high with you and the other kids at the stables."

Holly stood up and brushed herself off. "That's great."

Tess stood up, too, and they walked over to Buddy and Alice. "I really wanted to get acquainted with some of you kids before September, and I thought I could at Midtown. But I was scared nobody would like me."

Now Buddy and Alice eyed the carrot sticks in Tess's hand. "I think they want to share your food," Holly said.

Tess gave each horse a carrot stick, but neither was satisfied.

"I don't have any more carrots," Tess said.

"They don't care," Holly replied. "They'll eat your peanut-butter sandwich, too, if you let them. Some horses will eat almost anything and then get terrible cases of colic. They can be so greedy." She gave Buddy a hug around the neck.

"You know so much about horses," Tess said.

"Not as much as I should," Holly said, remembering her last practice session. "Guess we'd better head back to the barn. I have the center ring for half an hour this afternoon to practice pole bending, and I don't want to miss my turn. Come on, Chad."

He hurried up, hot and sweaty. "Do we have to go, Holly?"

"We'll come back another time," she said, gathering up the remains of their lunch.

"Tomorrow?" he asked.

"I can't promise for sure," Holly said.

Chad groaned. "It's so boring when you practice."

"Hey, Chad, I've got an idea," Tess said, patting Alice on the nose. "I don't have anything to do this afternoon. Why don't you hang out with me?"

"What'll we do?" he asked.

"It's going to be a surprise," Tess said.

"Neat," he shouted. "Let's go." He hurried over to his pony and untied him.

"Thanks, Tess," Holly whispered. She felt a sense of relief as they headed toward the stables. Now she could concentrate on Buddy without interruption. Now they'd really get somewhere. She just knew it.

6
Spoiled Little Kid

Several days later, Holly saddled Buddy in his stall, going over the last few practice sessions in her mind. Buddy just wasn't cooperating. He wouldn't follow orders and just generally acted like a spoiled little kid. If he had been a little kid, she would have recommended a spanking.

"Holly, Tess wants you to come watch her do something." Chad stood in the stall doorway, his new cowboy hat nearly covering his eyes.

"Sure thing." Holly gave his hat a yank and pulled it all the way down over his forehead. "Tell her I'm coming."

Chad took his hat off. "Cut it out," he said. Then he noticed Buddy's rabbit sitting on the corner shelf. "Can I play with the rabbit?"

"Afraid not," Holly said quickly. "If the rabbit got lost, or if anything else happened to it, Buddy would be very upset."

"Is Buddy kind of the way I was when I was little and had a blanket?" Chad asked.

Holly raised her eyebrows in surprise. "Hey, Chad, that's exactly right. The rabbit is Buddy's security pal, the way the blanket was yours."

"My mom says I'm too big to have a blanket now," Chad said. "And I think Buddy is too big for a rabbit." He put his hat on and left.

"Sometimes I think Chad's right, Buddy. Come on, it's time to work out." Holly led Buddy outside. She saw Tess standing next to Alice in the barnyard.

"Over here," Tess called.

Holly walked Buddy over to Tess. "I'm due in the ring right now," she said. "I can't go with you and Chad this afternoon."

"That's okay." Tess took off her glasses and wiped them on her shirt. "I can handle things myself now. Watch me."

"Okay." Holly watched as Tess put her left

hand on Alice's muzzle. Then she slid her hand along the horse's neck to the reins and picked them up. Next she raised her left foot and put it carefully in the stirrup. As she swung herself up, she grabbed the cantle, or back part of the saddle, with her right hand. She released the cantle when she eased her weight into the center of the saddle.

Tess looked down at Holly with a wide grin on her face. "How did I do, teacher?"

"Terrific mount," Holly said. And she really meant it. She couldn't believe this was the same Tess who had been so scared just a week and a half ago.

"Thanks," Tess replied. "Come on, cowboy," she called to Chad. "Let's hit the trail."

Holly watched Tess and Chad disappear down the trail, wishing in a way that she were going with them. She really wasn't looking forward to this afternoon at all. Mrs. Owens had asked for a preview of some of the girls' work, including hers, and she wasn't proud of her accomplishments.

"Come on, Buddy," she said, leading him to the center ring.

Judy and Karen and Mrs. Owens were already there. "Okay, Karen, let's see your pole-bending run," Mrs. Owens said.

Karen mounted her well-muscled quarter horse and guided him to the starting line near the row of six poles stuck in the ground.

"Go," shouted Mrs. Owens. Karen urged her horse to the poles, then ran him in a straight line down the right side of the row. At the last pole, she turned around and began to weave between each one, making her way back to the starting line. Then Karen turned her horse around and galloped toward the finish line at the other end of the poles.

"Good, Karen," Mrs. Owens called. "Come here and we'll talk about your performance."

Karen rode up to them and dismounted. "My timing was way off," she said breathlessly.

"No, it wasn't." Mrs. Owens smiled encouragement. "I think you need to direct your horse's head around the poles a little more. Give him more guidance so that he won't get out of position and begin hitting the poles." She paused and looked at Holly and Judy. "Any comments, girls?"

"I think Karen did very well," Holly said. She felt sure that Karen would get one of the pole-bending slots on the team.

"Okay, Holly, your turn." Mrs. Owens smiled down at her.

Holly took a deep breath as she mounted Buddy. She guided him to the starting line. Then she leaned over to pat his neck, whispering, "Now behave yourself, please."

"Go!" Mrs. Owens called.

Holly clicked Buddy into action, and he headed for the first pole. Just as she was ready to turn him into the weaving pattern, he reared. "No, Buddy," she said, fighting for control. He calmed down and reluctantly passed the first pole. Holly brought him toward the second. This time he stopped. "Go on, Buddy," Holly said, giving him a smack with her hand.

Now he pawed the ground with his right hoof. Did his leg hurt? Was he trying to decide whether to lead with his left or right front leg? Holly couldn't figure him out.

"Give him some help," Mrs. Owens called.

Holly dug her knees into Buddy's sides, and he suddenly started up again. But, instead of continuing around the next pole, he headed straight for Mrs. Owens at a gallop.

"Whoa," Holly called as Mrs. Owens took several steps backward. Buddy stopped just before running into her.

"I'm sorry," Holly said, as Mrs. Owens brushed dust from her jacket. "I guess this isn't Buddy's day."

Holly wanted to run away and cry. But she didn't. She went and sat on the sidelines and watched as Judy showed off her barrel-racing skills. Judy's bay gelding ran toward the three barrels centered in the ring, made tight turns around each of them, then returned to the starting line in the same way.

"Great, Judy," Mrs. Owens called, looking at

her stop watch. "That was excellent time. You can probably do a little better, though. Just don't give your horse so much rein until he gets all the way around each barrel. If you give him his head too soon, he'll run wide."

"Okay, thanks, Mrs. Owens," Judy said. "I'll try again later."

As Judy and Karen rode toward the barn, Holly turned to follow them.

"May I see you for a few minutes, Holly?" Mrs. Owens called, stopping her.

"I've watched you and Tess this past week," Mrs. Owens went on. "And I think it's wonderful how you've taught her some of the basics of horseback riding."

"Thank you," Holly murmured.

"But I think you'll have to spend more time with Buddy if you intend to be on the gymkhana team." Mrs. Owens smiled. "You're an excellent horsewoman."

"Thank you," Holly said again. "But I don't know what's wrong. Buddy won't do what I want him to do when we're out there in the center ring. On the trail he's okay, but in the ring where the poles are..." Holly swallowed a sob and fought to keep from crying.

"Let me see you try again."

Holly took Buddy through the poles once more while Mrs. Owens watched carefully.

When Holly had finished, Mrs. Owens said, "The way he's fighting you all the time, it's almost as if he's frightened of something. Have you ever taken part in any gymkhana events before? Did Buddy have an accident going around the poles at one time?"

"No, never." Holly shook her head. "This is his first gymkhana tryout."

Mrs. Owens put her arm around Holly's shoulder for a moment. "Keep trying," she said. "I'm sure you'll find out what's wrong and do a good job at the tryouts this Thursday." She patted Holly's shoulder, then turned and walked toward her office.

"I don't know, Buddy Boy," Holly whispered. "How can we possibly be ready on Thursday?"

7

A Scared Horse

"It's nice of Tess to invite some of you girls from the stables to have lunch at her house," Mrs. Flynn said as she drove Chad and Holly through the noontime traffic.

"I'm not a girl," Chad said.

"But you're a special friend of Tess, I understand." Mrs. Flynn smiled down at Chad, who was sitting beside her.

"Yep." Chad's cowboy hat almost hid his face. "We ride the range nearly every day."

Mrs. Flynn laughed and pulled up in front of Tess's house.

"We'll walk over to the stables after lunch, Mom," Holly said.

"Good. I'll pick you up about four o'clock," she said.

"Could you make that five?" Holly asked. "I've got to practice."

"Honey," Holly's mother began quietly. "Don't you think you ought to give it up? After all, gymkhana tryouts are the day after tomorrow."

"Don't worry, Aunt Martha," Chad said, giving her a hug. "I'll help Holly."

If only Chad *could* help, Holly thought as the two of them waved goodbye to her mother. They headed up the walk toward Tess's front door.

"Hi," Tess said in answer to their ring. "The other girls are here, and Mom's got the food about ready. We're going to eat outside on the picnic table." Her eyes danced behind her glasses. "Isn't this fun?"

Judy and Karen and a couple of other girls from the stables were out in the backyard playing with Frisbees. "Come on, Chad," Judy called. "Catch."

Everyone likes Chad, Holly thought, watching as the girls included him. And everyone likes Tess, too, now that they've gotten to know her. Holly watched as Tess paused to say something to Karen. Tess still was shy sometimes and didn't understand all the "horse talk" around the stables. But now she didn't care if the kids laughed once in a while. Tess knew it was all in fun.

"I'll go help your mother," Holly called.

She went into the kitchen and found Mrs. Bundy standing at the sink, rinsing some lettuce. "Hi," she said. "I'm Holly Flynn. Can I do anything to help?"

When Mrs. Bundy turned around, Holly couldn't believe her eyes. She knew she was staring, but she couldn't help it.

Mrs. Bundy began to smile. "Do I have a smudge on my nose?"

"Sorry," Holly said. "But for a second, I thought you were Aunt Helen."

"Oh, really?" Mrs. Bundy said. "And who is Aunt Helen?"

"Chad's mom," Holly said.

"Oh, yes, I've heard all about Chad," she said. "Tess thinks he's the nicest little boy in the world. I can't wait to meet him."

"I'll introduce you," Holly said. "Chad's outside."

Holly and Mrs. Bundy went outdoors.

"Chad," Holly called. "Come here."

When he saw Mrs. Bundy, he stood still for a moment. Then he began to run toward her. His cowboy hat flew off his head. Suddenly he stopped, and Holly could see the disappointment in his eyes.

"Hi, Chad," Mrs. Bundy said. "Tess has told me what good friends you've become." She bent down to shake his hand.

"I thought you were Mom." He stared at her, ignoring her hand.

"Sometimes that happens," Mrs. Bundy said. "Once I was walking down the street in a strange town, and I thought I saw my best friend." She smoothed his hair away from his face. "But my best friend was at home. Now, how about something to eat? Are you hungry, Chad?"

"No," he said and darted into the house.

"Chad," Holly shouted and began to run after him. But Mrs. Bundy put out her hand and held Holly's arm.

"Let him go, Holly," she said. "I'm sure he's missing his mother more than ever right now."

"Don't you think he needs me?"

"He may in a while," Mrs. Bundy said. "But right now, I think he needs to be alone. You talk to the other girls while I bring out lunch. And don't worry about Chad. I'll listen for him."

"Okay." Holly remembered that Mrs. Bundy was a kindergarten teacher, so she must know what she was doing. But still, it was hard to ignore little Chad and his feelings. He was a pest sometimes, but Holly really liked him a lot, and now she cared that he might be feeling miserable and lonely.

Mrs. Bundy brought out hot dogs and potato salad and a plate of brownies. She set them on a picnic table covered with a bright red cloth.

"Come on, everyone, let's eat," Tess said.

The other girls hurried up to the table and sat down, but Holly excused herself. "I'll be back in a minute," she said. She found Mrs. Bundy inside, fixing another plate of brownies. "Where's Chad?" Holly asked. "Doesn't he want lunch?"

"Perhaps if you asked him, he might come now," Mrs. Bundy said.

"Okay," Holly said. "Where is he?"

"In Tess's room." Mrs. Bundy pointed. "Through the hall, the first door on the right."

Holly found the door to the bedroom ajar. She peeked inside. "Chad?" she said quietly.

He was sitting in a chair by the bed, holding an old teddy bear that looked as if it had been Tess's when she was little.

"How's my favorite cousin?" Holly asked, sitting down on the bed and facing him.

"When am I going home?" he asked.

Holly tried to keep her voice light. "It won't be long now. Remember your dad said on the phone that your mom is doing well. She gets to leave the hospital sooner than the doctors had thought. You'll be going home in no time now, Chad."

He stared into the teddy bear's one remaining eye for a moment. Then he said, "Okay."

"You know what?" Holly said. "I'll bet Tess has had this bear as long as I've had my old rabbit."

"When did you give the rabbit to Buddy?" Chad asked.

"Last Christmas, when he seemed so sad. You know, he acted kind of scared and lonesome in his new home. And I had read all about horses needing mascots sometimes, so that's when I gave him my rabbit."

"Sometimes I wish I still had my blanket." Chad's voice was soft and small.

Holly looked at him with concern. "Maybe Tess will let you keep her teddy bear the rest of the time you're here. He can be your mascot."

"Do you think so?"

"Let's ask her, okay? Now, how about some food?"

"Okay. But first, I think I need a hug," Chad said. "But no kisses. I hate kisses."

"I promise." Holly laughed. "Just one hug." Then Chad stood up. He put his arms around her and hugged her hard. Poor little guy, Holly thought. He's really missed his folks and never said a word. He's tried to be so brave.

"Time's up for hugging," Chad said, setting the teddy bear on the bed. "Now let's eat."

They went outside, and Holly watched as Chad filled his plate with food. He ate everything quickly and then went back for seconds. But Holly only picked at her food. She was worried about Buddy.

"You're so quiet," Tess said later to Holly, as the others began to play with Frisbees again.

"It's Buddy," Holly said. "If I don't figure him out pretty soon, I may as well forget the gymkhana team."

"Do horses ever get scared?" Tess asked. "You know, the way I was scared?"

"Sure," Holly said. "When you take them some new place or..."

"Or when you try to get them to do something that's new?"

Holly looked at Tess. "That's it. That's it!"

"What is?" Tess said. "What are you talking about?"

"Buddy is scared of those poles in the center ring, and he needs his security blanket."

"Holly, have you flipped?" Tess asked.

"Yes... no... I don't know." Holly began to jump up and down. "I've got to go to the stables, Tess. Will you excuse me? Thanks for a wonderful time. I'll see you later. And thanks for telling me what's the matter with Buddy."

"What did I say?" Tess asked her. But Holly was already running across the lawn. Now she knew what to do about Buddy. Now she knew what had been wrong. Maybe there was still time to get ready for tryouts. There just had to be time. She was going to be on that team!

8
Lots of Ways to Win

And finally it was Thursday, the day of tryouts for the gymkhana team. Holly waited impatiently in Buddy's stall for the announcement of the pole-bending event. The barrel-racing tryouts were over and, according to the posted schedule, pole bending would be next. Any second now, Holly expected to hear Mrs. Owens's voice over the public address system, calling all the contestants to the center ring.

"Nervous?" Tess asked.

"Yes," Holly replied. "Scared, too." Now she understood how Tess had felt about riding horses and making friends. Now she could even sympathize with Buddy. He'd been scared of going into the center ring and trying something new. Simple as that. The problem wasn't his training. It wasn't his diet, or his health, or anything complicated. He'd just been scared and, if she'd been more aware, she could have solved the problem a long time ago, not just the day before yesterday, when it was almost too late.

"What are you thinking about?" Tess asked.

"How you were the one to tell me what was wrong with Buddy."

"I didn't tell you," Tess protested. "You figured it out for yourself and then knew what to do about it."

"I only figured it out after you asked me if horses ever get scared," Holly said. "I knew that Buddy's rabbit helped him when he first came to Midtown."

Holly smiled as she remembered what had happened two days ago. Then she went on. "And when I took the rabbit out to the center ring with Buddy, he settled down and began to work right away. He took one look at his rabbit and then began to turn the poles. He'd known how to do it all the time."

"Maybe one day I can enter one of the gymkhana events," Tess said. "Mom said I might get a horse for my birthday."

"Oh, Tess, that's terrific," Holly replied. "You're already becoming a good horseback rider."

"I never thought I'd hear that from anyone, ever." Tess laughed. Holly laughed, too, as she brushed Buddy's already gleaming coat.

Then she heard the announcement. "All pole benders report to the center ring to try out for the county fair gymkhana team," Mrs. Owens said.

"Oh, Tess." Holly's voice quivered.

"Come on," Tess said, smiling. "Once you're out there on Buddy, everything will be just fine."

"I hope so." Holly took his reins and led him outside. Tess followed, carrying the rabbit. Chad hurried toward them through the crowded barnyard.

"Hurry up, Holly," he said. His cowboy hat sat at an angle on his head. "You're number three in the competition. I asked Mrs. Owens."

Holly brushed his hair out of his eyes. "I'm sure going to miss you when you go home next week," she said.

"So am I," Tess said.

"Maybe you can visit me in Philadelphia," Chad said. "I'll let you play with my hamsters. I only had two when I left, but Dad says I have more now. Come on, Tess, sit with me and Aunt Martha."

"Thanks, Chad," Tess said. "But I have to stay and hold the rabbit for Buddy while he's performing."

"Will you always have to bring Buddy's rabbit when he enters a competition?" Chad asked. He scuffed his new cowboy boots in the dust.

"I don't think so," Holly said. "He'll get over being nervous about doing new things, I'm sure."

"The way certain people did," Tess added.

Chad's eyes danced. "Meaning you?"

"Meaning me," Tess replied. "I'll see you later partner, okay?"

"Okay." Chad pushed his way through the milling girls and horses and headed for the small spectator stand near the center ring.

"All contestants should go to the center-ring gate immediately," Mrs. Owens spoke into the public address system.

"Good luck," Tess whispered, as Holly mounted Buddy Boy. Then Holly walked him slowly to the ring and picked up her number card from the lady standing at the gate. "Wait right here," she said. "As soon as contestant number two is finished, you enter and proceed to the starting line."

"Thanks," Holly said, patting Buddy's back.

She watched as Karen, who was number one, put her horse through his paces. She made a great run, easily weaving in and out between the poles. When she returned to the starting line, she waved her cowboy hat to the spectators. They applauded enthusiastically.

Karen rode out of the arena as contestant number two began her run.

"You were great, Karen," Holly said. "And with that time, you're sure to win a place on the team."

"Hope so," Karen replied. "Hey, what did you do to Buddy? He seems like a completely different horse since Tuesday."

"Tess has the answer," Holly said, smiling mysteriously. "Watch her."

"Tess?" Karen's eyes were full of surprise.

When contestant number two finished, Mrs. Owens smiled at Holly. "This is it," Holly whispered to Buddy. "Do the best you can."

Buddy trotted into the center ring and stopped at the starting line. He eyed the crowd, snorting nervously and stomping a couple of times. Then Tess began to wave. She was holding the rabbit. Buddy seemed to see her standing at the far side of the ring.

"Ready, Holly?" Mrs. Owens called.

"Ready," she said. When the whistle blew, Holly tapped Buddy's sides with the heels of her boots, and they began their run at last. She could feel Buddy's sure stride under her as he began the initial run down the right side of the poles. He ran quickly and easily, and Holly kept herself in balance with his stride. She had the reins in her left hand, prepared to slide her free hand down to pull Buddy's head around the first pole, if necessary.

Now, as they neared the first pole, Holly let Buddy change his direction ever so slightly. He began making a wide circle, then closed in on the pole without actually touching it. Now he was in the proper position to start his weaving pattern.

They moved as a team, circling in and out of the poles. Holly forgot everything else but Buddy, concentrating hard on shifting her balance as he changed leads quickly and smoothly. In and out of the poles they moved, circling and moving toward the last one.

Now they were ready for the sprint to the finish line.

"Go, Buddy, go," Holly shouted, urging him

to move faster. And she could feel him respond. Could it be that Buddy was actually enjoying this? Maybe he wanted to win as much as she did.

"Come on, Buddy Boy," Holly shouted again.

Now the crowd was yelling and clapping. Holly could hear Chad's voice above everyone else's.

"Come on," he yelled.

Holly and Buddy crossed the finish line at last, and Holly reined Buddy to a stop in front of Mrs. Owens and the two other judges.

"Very good, Holly," Mrs. Owens said.

Holly guided Buddy quickly to the gate and dismounted in the stable yard. Tess and Chad hurried up to her.

"That was great!" Tess said. She hugged Buddy's sweaty neck.

"I know you won," Chad said, jumping up and down.

"We have to wait for the rest of the contestants to finish," Holly said. She knew her time was good, but was it good enough?

Five more girls tried out for the pole-bending event before Mrs. Owens and the other judges began to talk together. What were they talking about? What was taking so long? Finally, Mrs. Owens stepped to the microphone.

"Something unusual has happened today," she said. "As you know, I said there would be room for only two representatives of each event on the team that goes to the county fair. In pole bending, I will have to make an exception. We have a tie for second place. Karen Blair had the best time, so she will be ranked number one."

"Oh, Holly." Tess squeezed her friend's arm.

"However, Susan Summers and Holly Flynn tied with the second best time of the day, so we've decided that both of them will go to the fair."

Tess and Chad began to scream and dance around her, but for a moment, Holly only stood there, letting the joy of the moment sink inside her. She had made the team, after all. She felt happy, of course, but she'd felt almost as happy when she'd discovered what great people Tess and Chad were. Funny, she thought, there are lots of ways to win. Landing a place on the team is only one of them.

Chad looked up at her. "Well, don't just stand there. Say something."

"I left my speech at home," Holly said.

"That's okay," Chad said. "I can always talk, even if you can't."

Holly collapsed in laughter against Buddy, while Tess hugged and kissed Chad.

"Hey, no kissing," Chad shouted and ran through the crowd of horses and girls back to the spectator stand. Tess hurried after him.

"Come on, Buddy," Holly whispered. "You've earned a rest now." She took his reins and led him into the cool barn toward his stall.